The Seven Deadly Sins Of Love....

By Eric Orner

D1303285

St. Martin's Press
New York

ISBN 0-312-10539-8

First Edition: February 1994

10 9 8 7 6 5 4 3 2 1

For my lover, Stephen Parks
And for our Family, Victor and Lucy

Thanks also to my editor Keith Kahla, for sage advice, input, and hand-holding; to Ardys Jane Kozbial for sharp-eyed proofing; to Steffi Sommer for use of the hall; to my brother Peter; and to my mother, Rhoda Kaplan Pierce.

When I told a friend of mine I'd be writing the foreword for a book of gay cartoons, he looked puzzled. "Which cartoon strip is that?" he asked. "The only funny one," I replied. And he instantly knew which one.

For some reason—maybe the usual victimology syndrome, maybe the overly sensitive views of many editors in the gay press, maybe just bad luck—the vast majority of gay strips are either badly drawn or painfully earnest or both. Or they depict a stereotyped view of gay life, which died out (mercifully) some time in the early 1980s. Or their characters exist in a fantasy world that hardly reflects the complicated and often hilarious lives of most gay men and lesbians in America in the 1990s. Eric Orner's work is the glaring exception. Ethan, like most gay men, is mostly unfabulous, deeply conflicted, caught up in a gay culture that refuses to mesh very easily with the straight world that he also inhabits. He looks at the gym queens, p.c.-preachers, contorted Republicans, and hopelessly incorrect twentysomethings, and tries to make sense of them. He says in print what so many of us say in real life: Why do we search for the perfect lats when we're really looking for emotional security? Why do we love our often uncomprehending relatives? How do we get our relationships to last more than three weeks? Why can't we get over that boyfriend who tortured us? When will we act like grown-ups in our political activism? Were we genetically programmed without abdominal muscles?

Orner's work, like that of most of the best cartoonists, is journalism in the best sense of the word. It tells the truth; it tells it with unflinching accuracy and empathy. Because Ethan laughs at himself as well as at the world, he can tell us what others would never get away with: He can talk about the gulf between HIV-negative and HIV-positive men, while being fair to both; he can pinpoint the hypocrisy and bigotry of many straight Americans, while helping us see it through the lens of sympathy, rather than anger; he can mock the abstractions of activism, without ever seeming to denigrate the need to make progress. This is a real gift. And when Ethan cannot see reality, his cat can.

Enjoy this book. It's a work of a journalist a little ahead of his time: the sound of a confident, humane, funny voice that eventually more than gay America will come to appreciate.

Andrew Sullivan
The New Republic Magazine

The Seven Deadly Sins Of Love....

INTRODUCTION TO THE CHARACTERS

Ethan Green: The hero of these stories. He is dissatisfied with his job, his pecs, his clothes, his government, his hair, and most of the men he's been dating. Waging a perpetual quest for love...except for those times when love shows up, at which point the quest is called off while our hero waits for it to go away.

Lucy: Ethan's housecat, roommate, and Greek chorus. She knows all about the porn magazines under his bed, as well as the generally lackluster performances atop it.

Charlotte: Ethan's sharp-tongued next-door neighbor and soulmate.

The Hat Sisters: Smartly dressed divas, pleased to save all from hatred and homophobia, as long as it can be done before tea dance.

Bucky: Ethan's best friend. Unless either one is dating somebody.

Liza and Beth: Lovers for nine years, they do things like build successful businesses, wage political campaigns, and restore old Victorians, all while Ethan is off at brunch.

At closing time, the hungry eyes of geeky, sex starved desperados would dart furtively from guy to guy seeking one to take home.

The pickings were slim;

Bored couples looking to use your body for one night's sexual amusement..

Closeted Pentagon spokespersons..

Obscure First Lady Impersonators..

GOSH KNOWS EXACTLY HOW IT HAPPENED, BUT ETHAN GREEN FINDS HIMSELF INSIDE HIS OWN BRAIN..

TERRY'S MACHINE

OK... LET'S GET STARTED.. 4 EASY STEPS TO FINDING YOUR-SELF A LOVER BETWEEN, SAY, MIDNIGHT DECEMBER 22ND AND CHRISTMAS EVE.

STEP ONE: GO TO A CHRISTMAS TREE LOT. STEP TWO: IDENTIFY LONELY, SINGLE GUYS. (THEY'LL BE BUYING THOSE PATHETIC "OFFICE SIZED" MINI TREES).

SAY, THERE'S A HANDSOME ONE NOW...

SEASONS CHEERS ALAN & MARCI BUNBERG

HOW TO CATCH A MIDWEST MAN FOR THE HOLIDAYS IN FOUR

DISTURBING CARDS FROM MARRIED ELEMENTARY SCHOOL CLASSMATES..

STEP THREE: OFFER UP SOME GUARANTEED MIDWESTERNGUY© CONVERSATION.

"I SEE YOU'RE PURCHASING A TREE, BACK IN BOSHWEEGO COUNTY WE USED TO DECORATE OURS WITH SQUIRREL PELTS... ...GRANDMA USED TO DRIVE UP ON THE JOHN DEERE AND HOLLER MERRY.."

STEP FOUR: DON'T STAND ON CEREMONY.

DON'T LET THE SEASON TO BE MERRY BECOME THE SEASON TO BE MANLESS

SO, IF YOU DON'T HAVE PLANS, WOULD YOU LIKE TO COME OVER AND DRINK SPIKED EGGNOG & PUT ON PERRY COMO RECORDS & BUILD A FIRE AND ALLOW ME TO LICK EVERY INCH OF YOUR HARD HAIRY MUSCULAR BODY..

THAT'D BE SWELL

MIDWEST-ERNGUY-ANETICS

The ETHAN GREEN

GUIDE TO

BAD CABLE

PROGRAMMING;

Presents

*Point of reference: when not appearing in low rent comic strips, Williams works as the ass. sec. of defense for public affairs. The Washington Post says he's a talented tap-dancer.

FRESNO FELT THE OLD BATH-ROOM'S LAYOUT WAS INCON-VENIENT AT BEST...

> BUT FRESNO, LIZA AND BETH DISLIKE YOU DRINKING FROM THE TOILET...
>
> GET LOST FRESNO, OR I TELL 'EM YOU NEED A BATH..

AND HAVING TO CONSIDER THE ALMOND COLORED CARPETING *every* TIME HE FELT LIKE STRETCH-ING OUT ON THE LIVING-ROOM SOFA COULDN'T HAVE BEEN MORE IRRITATING.

AND LET'S NOT EVEN GET INTO HOW ANNOYING THOSE 2 FLIGHTS OF STAIRS COULD BE...

BETH... WHERE'R MY DOC MARTENS..?

OH SHIT..

So, "IT'S ABOUT FRIGGING TIME" FRESNO THOUGHT WHEN LIZA AND BETH *finally* WISED-UP AND BOUGHT HIM A BIGGER PLACE...

SIGH

SOLD SALE

WELL FRESNO SWEET BOY, HERE IT IS- YOUR NEW HOME!

NICE...

SO, WHERE WILL YOU TWO BE STAYING?..

WELL- I'D BETTER START PEEING ON THESE BUSHES..

Rules

For

Romance

Relapse

...

RULE #1B: AS PATHETIC AS YOU LOOK, THAT'S HOW TANNED & PUMPED & SNAPPILY DRESSED HE'LL LOOK...

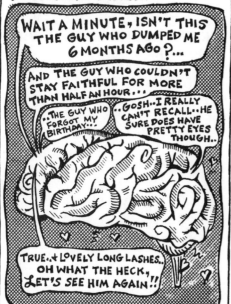

RULE #3: THE LITTLE MEMORY CHIPS INSIDE YOUR HEAD, WHOSE PURPOSE IT IS TO RECORD ALL OF THE MISERABLE THINGS HE EVER DID TO YOU, ARE SUDDENLY MALFUNCTIONING...

WAIT A MINUTE, ISN'T THIS THE GUY WHO DUMPED ME 6 MONTHS AGO?...

AND THE GUY WHO COULDN'T STAY FAITHFUL FOR MORE THAN HALF AN HOUR...

..THE GUY WHO FORGOT MY BIRTHDAY...

..GOSH..I REALLY CAN'T RECALL..HE SURE DOES HAVE PRETTY EYES THOUGH..

TRUE..+ LOVELY LONG LASHES.. OH WHAT THE HECK, LET'S SEE HIM AGAIN!!

RULE #4: YOUR FRIENDS WILL NOT BE ONE HUNDRED PERCENT SUPPORTIVE OF THESE DEVELOPMENTS.

YOU'RE GOING OUT WITH **WHO** SATURDAY NIGHT? ARE YOU FUCKING **NUTS**?

BETH

SWEETUMS?..ETHAN IS HERE.. SAYS HE'S GOING OUT WITH LEO AGAIN. I THINK HE MUST BE FEVERISH...

HATSISTERS

BUCKY

C'MON ETHAN, YOU KNOW WHAT A DICK LEO IS.. ON THE OTHER HAND HE'S GOTTA NICE BODY.. ..GREAT FOREARMS... ...AND THOSE EYES..HELL, WHY NOT SEE HIM AGAIN...

YOUR CAT

I WAS BORED BY THIS STRIP'S THEME BEFORE IT BEGAN..

CALL HIM ALREADY, LET'S GET IT OVER WITH...

I FEEL LIKE DELI.. WHERE'S THAT TAKEOUT NUMBER

LOVE'S
AFTERMATH
......

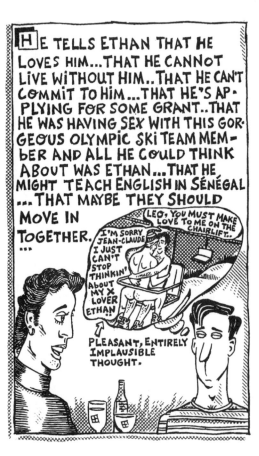

* "SO THEN CAMILLE PAGLIA SAID SOMETHING PROVOCATIVE AND EVERYONE WAS ABUZZ ABUZZ ABUZZ."

DINNER
PLANS
...

ONCE UPON a TIME, ON A SATURDAY EVENING, FIVE FRIENDS WERE MAKING PLANS TO DINE OUT...

the FIRST FRIEND DISLIKES THE THAI PLACE, THE FOOD THERE'S TOO SPICY FOR HIS PALATE, BESIDES, PARKING IS SUCH A HASSLE, BECAUSE THEY'VE GOT NO VAL-ET..

NO WAY ETHAN, THE LAST TIME WE WERE THERE IT TOOK THREE QUARTERS OF AN HOUR JUST TO FIND A PARKING SPOT, AND ANYWAY PEANUT SAUCES MAKE ME UNCOMFORTABLE...

the 2ND FRIEND SUGGESTED CAJUN, HE LOVES THE SHRIMP & CRAWFISH ettoufée BUT THE WAIT'S ALWAYS horrendous, AND THE CROWD'S NOT ALL THAT GAY.

I JUST KNEW WE SHOULD'A GONE TO THE "HARD ROCK"

YOU STRAIGHT PERSONS NEED TO TRY THE GUMBO..

I HATE THE CITY.

I Love THE PLACE, GIRLFRIEND, BUT NOT ON A SATURDAY NITE! IT ABSOLUTELY TEEMS WITH Suburbia..

the 3d FRIEND LIKES THIS NEW BISTRO, ON NORTHERN ITALIAN THEY ALL SEEM TO AGREE, ALAS, THEY WON'T EAT THERE THIS EVENING, #4 DISLIKES THEIR MAITRE d'.

the LACK OF PLAN CAUSED THE 5TH FRIEND TO GROW IRRITABLE, IN FACT ALL 5 SUDDENLY BECAME QUITE SURLY, SO THEY STAYED HOME SEPARATELY, AND ATE PASTA, GOT DEPRESSED AND WENT TO BED EARLY.

Ah, the holidays.. A time to relax,.. A time to enjoy home and hearth... A time to consider faking one's own death and moving under an assumed name to South America...

Campfire Girls

Your favorite sisters and mine were troubled by news reports detailing homophobia within local scouting programs. Feeling the need to investigate, but appreciating the delicate nature of any controversy involving youngsters, they went undercover;

BROWNIE?

OH PLEASE! CAMPFIRE GIRL...

Having volunteered at a nearby headquarters.....

WE'D LIKE TO BE DEN MOTHERS.

..The hat sisters were assigned spots as assistant troop leaders for an upcoming day trip up Mt. Stryker....

OK, OK ENOUGH "HUNDRED BOTTLES OF BEER ON THE WALL" WHO KNOWS SOMETHING BY SYLVESTER?

Now, as you might already know, Mount Stryker is the biggest of its kind in all of North America, perhaps in all of the world!.. Despite a bit of trepidation,

The Sisters conscientiously followed the Scout Master's instruction to bring up the hiking troop's rear.

As it happens, the Sisters did observe a clearly hostile attitude on the part of the Scout Master towards gay scouts...

(CONTINUED)

WELL, AS ANYONE WHO'S BEEN CAMPING (THE WOODSY KIND) WILL TELL YOU, IT ALWAYS RAINS. AND SURE ENOUGH, A SUDDEN STORM FORCED THE TROOP BACK DOWN TO THE SAFETY OF THEIR VAN..

NO FAGS IN SCOUTING I ALWAYS SAY, AIN'T THAT TRUE MEN?

SURE SARGE, WHAT-EVER..

HEY SARGE IT'S RAININ'

ONLY THING WAS, THE SCOUT MASTER HAD LOST THE KEYS... SEEMS HE HAD A LITTLE POCKET-KNIFE ON HIS KEY CHAIN THAT HE HAD BEEN USING AT LUNCHTIME TO CLIP HIS NAILS..

WAIT HERE, I'LL HAVE TO FUCKIN' HIKE BACK TO OUR FUCKIN' LUNCHSITE N' SEE IF I CAN'T FIND TH' FUCKIN' THINGS.

(end).

NOVEMBER, 1991;
BASKETBALL STAR
"MAGIC" JOHNSON
ANNOUNCES THAT HE
IS HIV POSITIVE.

id Winter
Blues...

TRYING TO FIGURE OUT IF YOUR NEW SIDEBURNS MAKE YOU LOOK LIKE A SEXY '90S GUY,.. OR MORE LIKE THAT JUNIOR DOCTOR ON MARCUS WELBY....

I'M SORRY, BUT LITTLE JEMMY HAS A RARE + INCURABLE DISEASE...WITH YOUR PERMISSION I'D LIKE TO TAKE HIM TO DISNEYLAND ON MY MOTORBIKE...

FEELING a LITTLE SILLY THAT YOU THOUGHT THAT THE 15 BUCKS YOU SENT THE CLINTON CAMPAIGN WAS AN ACT PREGNANT WITH POLITICAL SIGNIFICANCE...

WE DONATED $500!

BIG DEAL... MARYPAC, OF WHICH I'M TREASURER, GAVE 30G...

LOOK, THIS LAPEL PIN MAKES CLEAR HOW MUCH MORE IMPORTANT I AM THAN YOU...

DONELAN STATE PAC GIVES MORE THAN...

TRIANGLE BALL AT INAUGURAL

WONDERING HOW COME YOUR CAT HAS TAKEN TO WEARING THIS MORONIC RAVER'S CAP, AND SEEMS TO BE POPPING LOTS OF SUSPICIOUS PILLS...

(BLEAK)

GRIM

(SAME ONES.)

CAN I GO TO MONTRÉAL FOR THE WEEKEND?

HANDMADE FOR MARCH

THE HELLCAT...

SOMETIMES LUCY THE CAT MALICIOUSLY HYPNOTIZES ETHAN...

YOU'RE ON MIKONOS SUNBATHING... THE BEAUTIFUL SON OF A FORMER PRESIDENT LEANS OVER AND ASKS IF HE CAN BUY YOU A SOFT DRINK...

OFTEN THIS LEADS TO BIZARRE AND UNPRODUCTIVE CONDUCT...

TUNA CANNERY

HEH HEH HEH...

HAND OVER ALL THE CHUNK LIGHT TUNA IN SPRING WATER OR I WILL SHOOT

CANNERY FRONT OFF (NO CATS

HE DOESN'T APPEAR TO HAVE A GUN

MAYBE THEY'RE DIFFICULT TO SKETCH...

ENOUGH CHATTER, BRING ON THE FISH...

(CONTINUED)

FRANKLY, IF NOT FOR ETHAN'S RELIANCE ON THE KINDNESS OF STRANGERS, EPISODES LIKE THESE COULD TURN OUT MUCH UGLIER...

(end)

ETHAN'S IMAGE MAKE OVER.

(CONTINUED)

(end).

Finding

the "Gay" beach

while

on vacation...

RELAXING IN FRONT OF THE TV, ETHAN HAPPENS UPON THE MIDWESTERNGUY CHANNEL...

OK, SAY WHILE GROCERY SHOPPING YOU NOTICE A CUTE GUY:

- FIRST, WATCH WHAT HE SELECTS,
- THEN, SELECT EXACTLY THE SAME ITEMS.
- WHEN HIS ATTENTION'S DIVERTED, STEAL HIS SHOPPING CART.
- APOLOGETICALLY RETURN IT TO HIM.
- EXCLAIM ABOUT YOUR UNCANNY SIMILARITIES IN TASTE. ASK HIM TO DINNER IF HE DOESN'T ASK YOU FIRST...

WOW! WE BOTH BUY "I CAN'T BELIEVE IT'S NOT BUTTER" IN THE TUB!

EERIE! LET'S MAKE LOVE BEHIND THE DAIRY CASE, THEN I'LL TAKE YOU HOME TO MEET THE DOG..

OR, LET'S IMAGINE THAT IT'S THE HUNKY KID BEHIND THE BAKERY COUNTER WHO HAS YOUR HORMONES IN AN UPROAR,

- FIRST, TRY TO PURCHASE A RAISIN SCONE WITH A HUNDRED DOLLAR BILL.
- ANNOYED, THE HUNK WILL TELL YOU TO "JUST TAKE IT"...
- PROMISE TO COME BACK LATER & PAY.
- WHEN YOU DO, HE'LL BE CHARMED AND IMPRESSED BY YOUR DORKY HONESTY.

HELL MAYBE AN HONEST GUY WOULD BE A NICE CHANGE OF PACE..

HERE'S THAT BUCK I OWE YOU FROM YESTERDAY, GUY..

ARE YOU FREE FOR DINNER?

THE MIDWESTERNGUY® METHOD, DATES GALORE. ALMOST GUARANTEED!

I PROMISE YOU DATES GALORE!

Disturbing

Units

. . . .

LIZA AND BETH'S A.C. IS RELEASING MORE THAN ITS FAIR SHARE OF FLOUROCARBONS.

← OZONE

LIZA + BETH'S →

THE HAT SISTERS' WINDOW UNIT WAITS FOR OPPORTUNE MOMENTS, THEN PITCHES IT-SELF DOWN TO THE PAVEMENT..

GOOD GRACIOUS CONGRESSMAN DANNEMEYER— ARE YOU OK?

OOOOFF

ETHAN'S COOLING SYSTEM IS HOME TO A TINY LEPRECHUAN WHO URGES HIM TO ROB CONVENIENCE STORES...

ABOUT AN INCH TALL... TOTALLY GREEN... HE'S GOT A LITTLE APARTMENT BEHIND THE AIR FILTER... "GO AHEAD" HE SAYS, "HOLD UP THE SEVEN-ELEVEN..."

"YOU COULD EVEN DONATE SOME OF THE LOOT TO AIDS RESEARCH" HE SAYS..

"YOU WON'T GET CAUGHT" HE SAYS... "I PROMISE" HE SAYS..

Notes from the Beach.

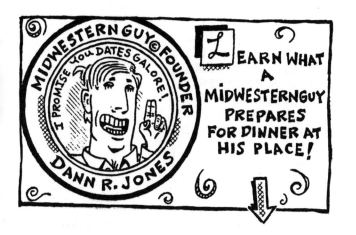

LEARN WHAT A MIDWESTERNGUY PREPARES FOR DINNER AT HIS PLACE!

GET KINDA DEEP AND MYSTICAL ABOUT CORN ON THE COB, + SERVE IT WITH EVERY MEAL..

THE INDIANS CONSIDERED CORN A GIFT FROM THE SUN GOD. OUR PIONEER ANCESTORS BUILT WHOLE TOWNS OUT OF USED COBS..

HE'S SO REAL!

(CONTINUED)

MAKE HOMEMADE MACARONI + CHEESE, BUT BURN IT AND THEN "CUSS" A LOT.. ENDEARING HELPLESSNESS IN THE KITCHEN APPEALS TO LOTS OF GUYS.

OH "SHOOT"

GOD HE'S SOOOO CUTE

So YOU'RE AT ANOTHER MEMORIAL SERVICE FOR ANOTHER FRIEND WHO SHOULD'VE DIED IN MAYBE THE 2010's or 2020's.

AND YOU'RE REMEMBERING CHUCKLES THE CLOWN'S FUNERAL ON THE MARY TYLER MOORE SHOW & WISHING YOU FELT LIKE GIGGLING RATHER THAN SITTING HERE ALL SHELLSHOCKED AND PISSED AND BLEARY-EYED WONDERING WHO YOU'LL BE SITTING HERE FOR NEXT TIME. AND YOU'RE MAKING A MENTAL NOTE TO BE HOSTILE TO YOUR FATHER BECAUSE HE SENDS MONEY TO REPUBLICANS.

BASICALLY-INTELLIGENT, OTHERWISE-NORMAL-DAD.

TEST #1
HATE FILLED RIGHT WING FUNDAMENTALIST RULE OF PLANET.

FRIGHT-O-METER®

TEST #2
PENNY-A-GALLON GAS TAX

YAWN

YOUR HEAD HURTS BECAUSE YOU'VE BEEN DRINKING a SCARY AMOUNT,... AND POPPING BEN- adryl (THE ONLY THING YOU HAD IN THE HOUSE) SO YOU COULD SLEEP...

AND YOU WONDER IF MICHAEL IS A GRAIN OF SAND NOW, OR A STREAM, OR A DISTURBANCE IN SOME PEARLY GATES PROCESSING LINE...

THANKS TO STEPHEN PARKS

AN AGING
TELEVISION
PERSONALITY
AND I
FELL
DEEPLY
IN
LOVE...

✱ "ALL ABOUT EVE"!.

UNFABULOUSLY, YOU FIND YOURSELF ON A DATE WITH A GUY WHO ONLY TALKS IN NON-SEQUITURS..

So, CAL & BOBBY BOUGHT A TIME SHARE ON ST. MARTIN WHICH WAS FABULOUS UNTIL CAL FINALLY GOT THERE AND SAW THE WHOLE PLACE WAS DONE IN THIS **TACKY** WALNUT AND JUST TOTALLY **FREAKED** AND ABSOLUTELY INSISTED ON REPAPERING BEFORE HE'D EVEN CONSIDER LOOKING AT THE BEACH.

HAVE I TOLD YOU ABOUT MY YORKIES?

TRYING TO RECALL WHO SET HIM UP ON THIS DATE SO HE CAN SLASH THEIR TIRES...

...YOUR THOUGHTS DRIFT OFF TO A FANTASY BOYFRIEND...... THE TWO OF YOU LIVE IN A TINY APARTMENT IN ROME OR RIO, OR CHELSEA... HE'S SOME STRANGE ETHNIC HYBRID-JEWISH INDONESIAN.. HIS NAME'S DOM, HIS MOM'S AN AGING EXOTIC DANCER IN BAYONNE, NEW JERSEY. HIS DAD'S A HIGH-RANKING DIP- LOMAT FROM BORNEO. HE'S A POET WITH ROUND GLASSES AND WILD HAIR & A SKINNY BODY AND INCREDIBLY SENSUAL LIPS...

... AND WHEN YOU RETURN TO YOUR FLAT AT NIGHT HE GREETS YOU AT THE DOOR COMPLETELY NAKED WITH A BOWL OF SPICY THAI NOODLES (AND AN ERECTION) ... ONE DAY THE INTENSITY OF YOUR RELATIONSHIP BECOMES TOO MUCH TO BEAR. YOU LEAVE

NOTE: THIS BEING A FANTASY, YOU GET TO WEAR A COOL ITALIAN SUIT

HIM FOR CURT, OR DIRK OR HAL A HOUSE PAINTER FROM DELAWARE, WHO DRINKS YUENGLING, HASN'T TOLD HIS 9 BROTHERS & SISTERS THAT HE'S GAY, AND LIKES TO MAKE LOVE TO YOU ON THE FRONT LAWNS OF THE JOBS HE'S WORKING ON ....

CURT, DIRK OR HAL INC. HOUSE PAINTING (80   69

.. AND YOU CAN BET HIS PANTIES WERE IN A BUN— HEY... I GET THE FEELING YOU'RE NOT EVEN LISTENING! HELLO? EHEM...

CONFUSED? BEWILDERED?

Just pretty-much ABsolutely uncertain?

Then,

WHY NOT EMPLOY THE LABORATORY-TESTED, 4-STEP, GUARANTEED, ETHAN GREEN METHOD FOR DETERMINING THE SEXUAL PREFERENCE OF YOUR NEW *Boss...*

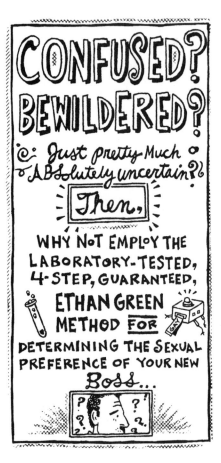

STEP ONE:

OBSERVE THE LITTLE THINGS CAREFULLY...

★ DOES HE SQUARE THINGS OFF ON HIS DESK?...

★ DOES HE EAT CAESAR SALADS AT LUNCH?.. — CROUTON

★ DOES HE HAVE FRAMED PICTURES OF PETS ON HIS DESK? — Fi Fi

★ DOES HE BRING A GYM BAG TO WORK?...

 **TEP TWO:**

SURVEILLANCE...

FOLLOW HIM ON SATURDAY AFTERNOON. WATCH CAREFULLY TO SEE IF HE APPEARS IN TRENDIER NEIGHBORHOODS CARRYING CRATE & BARREL PACKAGES...

GIRLFRIEND - HOW'R WE DOING?

HI HANQUE, I'D LIKE A CAPUCCINO AND SOME LOBSTER BISQUE...

Crate

(FRIENDLINESS WITH THE WAITSTAFF IS A GOOD SIGN)

TEP THREE:

GO OUT ON A LIMB...

VOLUNTEER TO STAY LATE HELPING HIM WORK ON THAT SPECIAL PROJECT...

Y'KNOW ETHAN, I REALLY APPRECIATE YOUR STAYING AND HELPING ME OUT TONITE.. I DON'T KNOW WHAT I'D DO WITHOUT YOU...

NO PROBLEM, DOUG..

WOW, I'M REALLY BEAT...

TEP FOUR:

MENTION HIS SHOULDERS LOOK A BIT TIGHT...

UM... DOUG?... WANT A MASSAGE?...

← DRAMATIC EFFECT

THE SEVEN DEADLY SINS OF LOVE.

(CONTINUED)

THE SEVEN DEADLY SINS OF LOVE.

(END).

@RELATIONSHIP
CONSULT
WITH
MADAME ZOLNA;

E-Z

WEDDING

GUIDE

— FOR —

GAY

PEOPLE

.

1. OK, SO FIRST OF ALL, YOU GET ANOTHER ONE OF THESE AWFUL INVITES...

"DR. AND MRS. DONALD PHIFFENBACHER REQUEST YOUR PRESENCE AT THE WEDDING OF THEIR DAUGHTER JUDYTHE-LYNNE AT ONE AND THIRTY O'CLOCK BLAH BLAH

2. IF YOU'RE REALLY LUCKY, IT'LL BE FROM SOMEBODY YOU LIKE...

YOUR COOL STRAIGHT-COUPLE NEIGHBORS

WE'RE GETTING MARRIED IN THE BACK YARD. BRING A CASSEROLE AND A LOVER..

3. MORE THAN LIKELY, HOWEVER, THE WEDDING THAT YOU'RE BEING SUMMONED TO IS THAT OF;

(a) SOME LONG-FORGOTTEN COLLEGE HOUSEMATE.

(b) A MENTALLY IMPAIRED SECOND COUSIN.

(c) A NERDY OFFICE CO-WORKER.

REMEMBER THAT YEAR I DRANK TOO MUCH N' BARFED EVERY DAY! WHAT A GAS!! 'GIGGLE'

REMEMBER THAT 4TH OF JULY WE PLAYED SOFTBALL? WHERE DIDJA' GET THAT SUCKY ARM?! SNICKER

REMEMBER OUR LAST AUTOMATED VOICE MAIL SYSTEM BOY WHAT A CLUNKER!

HAW

MENSA I AIN'TSA

4. AND SINCE THESE FOLKS WOULDN'T INVITE YOUR LOVER EVEN IF YOU HAD ONE, YOU'RE GETTING A LITTLE DEPRESSED.

WELL,.. A LITTLE NAUSEOUS MAYBE..

DON'T BE SILLY, I ALWAYS ENJOY A GET-TOGETHER WITH LOTSA FAMILY VALUES..

NOT TO MENTION BAD DANCING..

5. WELL HEY, WHY NOT MAKE YOUR-SELF A *LITTLE* DEAL;

WHEN THE STRAIGHT PEOPLE IN YOUR *LIFE* CELEBRATE YOUR RELATIONSHIP, CELEBRATE THEIRS. WHEN THEY DON'T, FIRST, CHUCK THE INVITATION, THEN..

GO AHEAD BOY, CHEW IT UP..

6. ..SEND A CHEAP GIFT..

COASTERS WITH "I LUV A PARTY" PRINTED IN TASTE-FUL SCRIPT

SOAPS

FLORIDA SOUVENIR

G*!*!

ETHAN DOLL WITH SUCTION CUPS FOR CAR WINDOW

...AND SPEND THE DAY OF THE WEDDING INDULGING IN PETTY BUT UPLIFTING THOUGHT...

o o o o o o o o

STRAIGHT PEOPLE AGE SO POORLY... AND THEIR FASHION SENSE? *PLEASE*..

DIDN'T JUST THAT SORT OF BEHAVIOR GET ME YELLED AT LAST WEEK!

★ GREAT LAKES SISTERS ★

YOUR FAVORITE SISTERS & MINE WERE WORKING ON THEIR MEMORIAL DAY OUTFITS WHEN THEY RECEIVED AN UPSETTING CALL...

CUPCAKE, WHENEVER YOU FINISH DROOLING WE CAN GET TO WORK ON OUR MEMORIAL DAY OUTFITS..

I'LL PENCIL YOU IN FOR NEXT MONTH...

APPARENTLY THE "LIBERAL" MAYOR OF MILWAUKEE WISCONSIN WAS WORRIED ABOUT RE-ELECTION. AND ALTHOUGH HE WAS FIRST ELECTED WITH LOTS OF GAY SUPPORT, HE FELT THAT BEING OUR FRIEND MIGHT BE A LIABILITY IN HIS CURRENT RACE AGAINST A FEW RIGHT-WING CRAZIES... SO HE DECIDED TO DUMP ON GAYS A BIT, FIGURING THEY HAD NOWHERE ELSE TO GO...

VOTERS'LL ASSOCIATE GAYS WITH DAHMER — BETTER CANCEL THE PRIDE PARADE..

Now, the sisters don't like Wisconsin much, because the butter fat content of ice cream there poses a nasty challenge to their dietary efforts.. Nevertheless they felt Gay Milwaukee needed a lift.

WE'LL BE THERE AS SOON AS WE CAN

HOW 'BOUT A WALK, HATDOG..

So they dressed in something suitably Germanic..

DRIVER, WISCONSIN PLEASE.

JUST TAKE US TO THE AIRPORT..

TAXI

YESMAMS..

(CONTINUED)

(end).

COUNTDOWN

TO

LOVE

WELCOME TO **PINK PAWS**. GUARANTEED TO SEPARATE NEUROTIC GAY PET OWNERS FROM EVERY LAST DOLLAR OF DISPOSABLE INCOME.

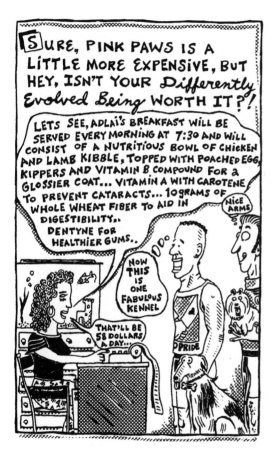

HOLIDAY TRAUMA
REVISITED

IF OUR FAVORITE SiSTERS CAN BE FAULTED AT ALL, (& I'M INCLINED TO BELIEVE THEY CAN'T BE) IT'S SIMPLY BECAUSE THEY CARE ABOUT PEOPLE TOO MUCH... SO IT'S NOT HARD TO UNDERSTAND JUST HOW BADLY THEY FELT UPON LEARNING THAT 2 DEAR OLD FRIENDS FROM L.A. WERE TREATING EACH OTHER TERRIBLY, AND WERE ON THE VERGE OF SPLITTING UP...

THE TRAGIC REPORTS PROVED TRUE, RELATIONS WERE BADLY FRAYED...

AND SO THE HAT SISTERS TRIED EVERYTHING THEY COULD THINK OF TO EFFECT A RECONCILIATION... BUT THE COMBATANTS WOULD HAVE NOTHING OF IT... A MRS. BATES, WHO LIVED NEARBY, TOLD OUR HEROINES THAT THIS HAD BEEN GOING ON FOR QUITE SOME TIME...

JANE, YOU'VE COMMITTED AN ACT OF UNKINDNESS...

SAY, HOW ABOUT A TRIP TO THE BEACH?

YOU SAID COOK HER SOME DIN-DIN SO I DID... I COOKED HER SOME DIN-DIN...

JANE DEAR, UNGAG YOUR SISTER...SHE'S TURNING PURPLE.

PAN FRIED PET CANARY (WITH BASIL)

WELL, IT'S SAD TO SAY, BUT THE SISTERS LEARNED, AS WE ALL DO AT SOME POINT IN OUR LIVES, THAT SOME PEOPLE JUST DON'T WANT TO BE HELPED.

THERE NOW! ISN'T THIS OODLES BETTER! I JUST KNEW A TRIP TO THE SEA SHORE WOULD HELP PATCH THINGS UP... ISN'T THIS GORGEOUS!

OOOH I HATE IT WHEN IT'S NOT MY TURN TO BE ANNETTE..

I LIED. YOU WEREN'T THE CAUSE OF MY PARALYZING ACCIDENT..

WHY YOU BITCH!!

YOU DID, HOWEVER, RUN UP A STAGGERING LIQUOR TAB AT JOHNSON'S, ...NOT TO MENTION YOUR BLUDGEONING TO DEATH OF OUR HOUSEKEEPER, ELVIRA, YOUR SURLY DEMEANOR,... YOUR INCESSANTLY OFF KEY SINGING..

GOLDEN GLOBE

THE

ETHAN GREEN

GUIDE

TO

Pee Shyness

...

FEAR AND **L**OATHING
at the
LESBIAN, BISEXUAL & GAY
ALLIANCE
• • •

SO IT'S FRIDAY NIGHT AND YOU AND YOUR NEW BOYFRIEND FIND YOURSELVES TRAPPED IN THE "I-DUNNO-WHAT-DO-YOU-FEEL-LIKE-DOING?" VORTEX...

MOVIE?

NAHH...

NAHHH...

INDIAN FOOD?

NAHH..

DANCE CLUB?

WHY NOT BREAK OUT BY FIXING HIM A DINNER SURPRISE..

WOW! A PERSONALIZED LASASAGNA-

OH SWEETHEART IT'S WONDERFUL- WE CAN'T EAT IT- I WANT IT BRONZED.. CALL MY MOM- WE'LL HAVE THE GUY WHO DID MY BABYSHOES COME FETCH IT...

IT'S HANDCUT ALPHABET PASTA- CREMALDI'S HAD IT ON SALE..

(CONTINUED)..

ASTONISHINGLY, YOU AWOKE TO FIND YOUR-SELF CAUGHT UP IN THE BRISTLES OF A MAMMOTH HAIRBRUSH...

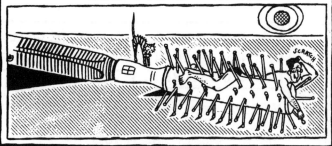

IT MADE NO SENSE AT ALL, REALLY NOT 1 IOTA... BUT THE IMPLICATION WAS CLEAR, YOU WERE STRANDED... STRANDED IN THE

LAND OF THE GIANT QUEENS.

(CONTINUED)

MAKING YOURSELF PRESENTABLE PROVED PROBLEMATIC... YOUR PLAN TO UTILIZE AVAILABLE HAIR CARE PRODUCTS, UNSUCCESSFUL.

AS FOR THE GQs THEMSELVES, WELL, TWO OF THEM WERE IN THE LIVING ROOM, PRACTICING POSTURE ...

MY GAWD HAS NO ONE TAUGHT YOU TO STAND PROPERLY?

NO. NO. NO.. WEIGHT ON THE LEFT HEEL! NOW WAVE AND TOUCH PEARLS.. NOW POINT TOES.. NO NO NO.. THE TOES THE TOES ... OY,... YOU JUST CAN'T FIND A GOOD AU PAIR NOWDAYS. BALANCE DEAR.. CONTRAPPOSTO... THIS IS GIVING MOTHER SUCH A HEADACHE...

A THIRD CRITIQUED FROM THE SIDELINES AS SHE FIXED HERSELF A GIANT COCKTAIL...

TRY WALKING, DEAR, THINK PEBBLE BETWEEN THE CHEEKS.. NO.. TOO SLOPPY.. THINK DIME BETWEEN THE CHEEKS...

Y OU KNEW THAT YOU SHOULD ESCAPE, THAT'S PRETTY MUCH STANDARD OPERATING PROCEDURE FOR FICTIONAL HEROES WHO FIND THEMSELVES AMONG HUGE (& BITCHY) BEINGS... ... BUT YOU KINDA' WANTED TO STICK AROUND AND TRY ON ONE OF THEIR GIANT FREDERICK'S OF HOLLYWOOD PUMPS...

MY MY, WHAT WE LEARN ABOUT OURSELVES IF WE LIVE LONG ENOUGH...

LIVE LONG ENOUGH? BUT I'M ONLY 21...

YEA, AND I'M ONE OF THE LION CUBS FROM "BORN FREE"...

CLOMP

PARK

GAY MAN'S TAKE ON JURASSIC

(END).

I COULD INFECT HIM.. SHIT.. I COULD KILL HIM STOP!

You've DISCUSSED THIS. You've AGREED TO TAKE THINGS A DAY AT A TIME.. START THINKING THIS WAY 'N THERE'LL BE NOTHING TO TAKE... TRY AND FOCUS ON THE MOVIE...

I ALWAYS ASSUMED BEING A COUPLE—BEING WITH SOME-ONE—MEANT SHARING YOURSELF WHOLLY, ... ENTIRELY... BUT HOW CAN I SHARE *THIS* ENTIRELY AND BE NEGATIVE?.. HE'LL THINK I CAN'T UNDERSTAND.. MAYBE I CAN'T...

..I'M OBSESSING..

C'MON.. YOU AGREED TO GO SLOWLY.. SO CHILL.. EAT S'MORE PIZZA.. GET YOUR MIND OFF THIS..

AFTER A RESPECTABLE PASSAGE OF MOMENTS...

WATCHING DANIEL DAY-LEWIS RUN AROUND THE ADIRONDACKS IN A LOIN CLOTH IS MAKING ME HORNY..

WATCHING DANIEL DAY-LEWIS RUN AROUND THE ADIRONDACKS IN A LOIN CLOTH IS MAKING ME HORNY..

MMMMM... YOU TASTE GOOD...

YOU TASTE GOOD. I TASTE LIKE PEPPERONI, LEMME GO BRUSH MY TEETH...

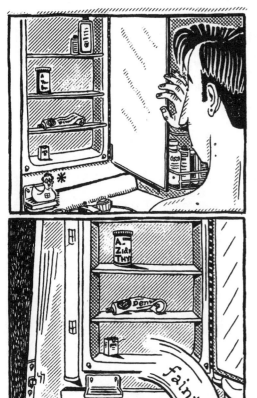

* SAM NUNN BATHDUCK
FOR THOSE WASHTIME
DROWNINGS...

(CONTINUED)

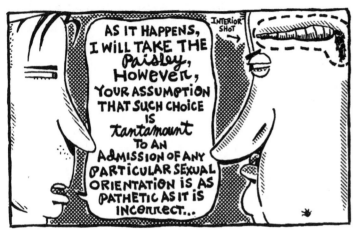

(End).

(CONTINUED)

WISE CRACKS SPARED YOU FROM THE WORST FATE OFFERED BY PICKING TEAMS.. ..OTHERS WEREN'T SO LUCKY...

LEMME SEE, TWO RETARDS LEFT...

HMMM... I'LL TAKE GREEN... AT LEAST HE'S A FUNNY RETARD, AINTCHA GREEN, HEY DO THAT "HORSHAK" IMPRESSION...

IRONICALLY, YEARS LATER, SOMEWHERE ON THIS EARTH YOUR OLD TORMENTORS CAN'T GET UP A FLIGHT OF STAIRS WITHOUT *Wheezing*, WHILE YOU SPEND 5 NIGHTS A WEEK DEVELOPING YOUR "TRAPS"...

UP UP UP

SOLVO ATLANTA

UP UP UP

NEEDLESS TO SAY, STAIRS AREN'T THIS *only* PROBLEM

A LITTLE CAREER CRISIS..

WHEN LAST VISITED, ETHAN & DOUG'S BUDDING ROMANCE HAD COLLIDED WITH THE REALITY OF DOUG'S SEROPOSITIVE STATUS... THE INTERVENING WEEKS HAVE SEEN...

(Continued)

Among the publications in which *The Mostly Unfabulous Social Life of Ethan Green* appears regularly are:

Bay Windows (Boston MA.)
The Washington Blade
San Fransico Bay Times
Southern Voice (Atlanta)
The Pink Paper (London)
Xtra (Toronto)
The Texas Triangle
Equal Times (Minneapolis)
The Windy City Times (Chicago)
Gaybeat (Columbus)
St. Louis Gay News Telegraph

Front Page (Raleigh)
Twist Weekly (Seattle)
The Cleveland Gay People's Chronicle
Our Paper (Portland, ME)
The Latest Issue (Sacramento)
Baltimore Gay Paper
Query (Nashville)
The Weekly News (Miami)
Philadelphia Gay News
Out (Pittsburgh)
Genre (Los Angeles)

It is my great privilege to work with support staffers, reporters, editors, and publishers who sacrifice much in providing us with the means to talk to each other.

Eric Orner
September '93

BIOGRAPHY

Eric Orner has been writing the Ethan Green saga since 1989. Since then, tales of Ethan's mostly unfabulous social life have appeared in about fifty gay, lesbian, and progressive newspapers across the United States, Canada, and Great Britian.

Eric Orner lives and works in Cambridge, Massachusetts, a place he admires. Many of the cartoon stories in this book were written in Provincetown, Massachusetts, a place he loves.